BLACKTIP SHARK

Madeline Nixon

www.av2books.com

Step 1
Go to **www.av2books.com**

Step 2
Enter this unique code
FRTNY89GI

Step 3
Explore your interactive eBook!

AV2 is optimized for use on any device

Your interactive eBook comes with...

Contents
Browse a live contents page to easily navigate through resources

Audio
Listen to sections of the book read aloud

Videos
Watch informative video clips

Weblinks
Gain additional information for research

Try This!
Complete activities and hands-on experiments

Key Words
Study vocabulary, and complete a matching word activity

Quizzes
Test your knowledge

Slideshows
View images and captions

... and much, much more!

CONTENTS

What Is a Blacktip Shark?

Blacktip sharks get their name from their color. The tips of their **fins** are black. Blacktip sharks have bodies shaped like **torpedoes**. Like all sharks, their skin is different from that of other fish. Instead of scales, they have **denticles**. This helps blacktip sharks move quickly through the water.

"Sharks are among the most perfectly constructed creatures in nature. Some forms have survived for two hundred million years."

—Eugenia Clark, 'The Shark Lady', Scientist, Shark Behaviorist, and Marine Conservationist

Blacktip Shark

Scientific Name *Carcharhinus limbatus*

Diet Carnivore

Size 5–8 feet (1.5–2.4 meters)

Weight 66–220 pounds (30–100 kilograms)

Conservation Status Near threatened

Population Unknown

Blacktip Shark Features

Blacktip sharks have features that help them live. Some help them find and catch food. Others help them to eat food once they catch it.

Snout
A blacktip shark has special **cells** on its snout. They are called **electroreceptors**. These cells help the shark find other animals.

Teeth
The teeth of a blacktip shark are long, sharp, and jagged. They help the shark tear apart its food.

Body
The body of a blacktip shark is **streamlined**. This allows the shark to jump out of the water and spin.

Blacktip Shark Life Cycle

Every two years, female blacktip sharks give birth to live babies. These young sharks are called pups. When they are born, pups are only about 13 to 26 inches (33 to 66 centimeters) long. They spend their early years in shallow waters away from large **predators** and big boats. Blacktip sharks live about 12 years.

How Big Are Sharks?

Human
5.5 feet (1.7 m)

Blacktip Shark
8 feet (2.4 m)

Bull Shark
11.5 feet (3.5 m)

Shortfin Mako Shark
12 feet (3.7 m)

Tiger Shark
16 feet (4.9 m)

Great Hammerhead Shark
20 feet (6.1 m)

Great White Shark
20 feet (6.1 m)

Whale Shark
32 feet (9.8 m)

The oldest known blacktip shark was a 15.5-year-old female.

Life in the Ocean

Blacktip sharks usually live in warm waters. They stay there during winter months. However, they have been spotted in colder waters during the summer. Blacktip sharks spend most of their lives close to shore. There, they hunt schools of fish. Blacktip sharks often come across humans and boats.

SHARK BITES
Female blacktip sharks are heavier than **males**.

Blacktip Sharks around the World

Blacktip sharks live mostly in the Gulf of Mexico and the Caribbean Sea. They are **coastal** sharks. This means they are not found in the open ocean.

LEGEND Blacktip Shark Range Land Water

1 Galapagos Islands, Ecuador

Blacktip sharks live near **reefs** in the Galapagos Islands year round. There are many types of fish here for them to eat.

2 Palm Beach, Florida

Thousands of blacktip sharks come to Florida around mid-January. Here, the waters are warmer than in the northern United States.

3 Thevenard Island, Australia

The water off Thevenard Island, Australia, is the perfect temperature for blacktip sharks. They do not go further than about 492 feet (150 m) from shore.

Finding Food

Blacktip sharks eat only meat. This makes them **carnivores**. They eat different types of fish. Some of the fish they feed on are small. Others are larger fish such as catfish, triggerfish, and flatfish. Blacktip sharks also eat stingrays, squids, and smaller sharks. Blacktip sharks sometimes follow fishing boats. They wait for fishers to throw away fish they do not want to keep.

Blacktip sharks hunt at great speeds. They attack from below and snap their jaws while swimming. This causes them to jump and spin out of the water.

SHARK BITES
A blacktip shark has **15 rows of teeth** in each jaw.

Blacktip Shark History

Achille Valenciennes was a French **zoologist.** He first discovered the blacktip shark in 1839. However, they have been around for about 23 million years. Today, blacktip sharks are very common. They can be found worldwide.

The blacktip shark's scientific name means "sharp nose and bordered fins."

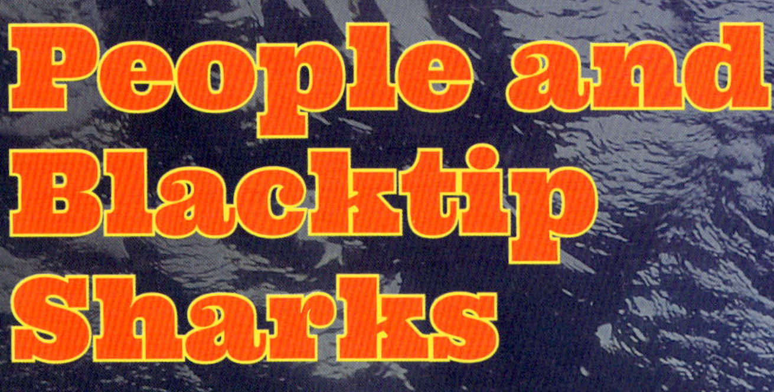

People and Blacktip Sharks

Blacktip sharks are curious but shy. They do not attack unless **provoked**. These sharks do not usually bite humans. When they do, it is because they mistake people for prey.

Swimmers and fishers often see these sharks because they live close to shore. Sometimes, fishers accidentally catch them. Blacktip sharks mostly stay away from humans unless they are feeding. This makes it hard to study them.

SHARK BITES

Since the 1950s, blacktip sharks have **bitten** about **30** people in **Florida**. Most of these **bites** were **minor**.

The blacktip shark was declared near threatened in 2005. Their numbers had dropped since 2000.

Protecting Blacktip Sharks

Bull sharks and tiger sharks are the main predators of blacktip sharks. Humans also hunt them for their meat. Blacktip shark fins are used as food in Asia. Their **hides** can also be used for leather.

There are rules against the overfishing of blacktip sharks. However, some fishers break these rules. In the United States and Australia, blacktip sharks are protected by law.

Blacktip Shark Conservation Status

Test Your Knowledge

1

Which two sharks eat blacktip sharks?

Bull sharks and tiger sharks

2

What are the special cells in a blacktip shark's snout called?

Electroreceptors

3

Which scientist discovered blacktip sharks?

Achille Valenciennes

4

When was the first blacktip shark discovered?

1839

5

Why do blacktip sharks follow fishing boats?

To catch fish fishers throw away

6

How old was the oldest recorded blacktip shark?

15.5 years old

7

Where do thousands of blacktip sharks migrate during mid-January?

Palm Beach, Florida

8

What is the scientific name for blacktip sharks?

Carcharhinus limbatus

Key Words

carnivores: animals that eat meat

cells: the smallest units of living things

coastal: near the shore

denticles: tough tooth-like scales that cover a shark's skin

electroreceptors: cells in a shark's snout that help it find prey

fins: the thin parts of a fish's body that help it swim

hides: the skins of animals treated and used for fashion, decoration, or warmth

predators: animals that kill and eat other animals

provoked: made angry

reefs: the materials just below the water's surface made up of coral, rock, or sand

streamlined: made smooth, making it easy to move through water or air

torpedoes: long, oval-shaped objects that travel in water

zoologist: a person who studies the animal kingdom

Index

Get the best of both worlds.

AV2 bridges the gap between print and digital.

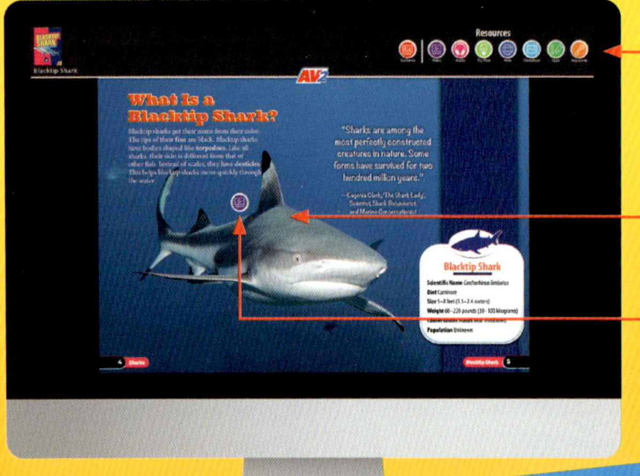

The expandable resources toolbar enables quick access to content including **videos**, **audio**, **activities**, **weblinks**, **slideshows**, **quizzes**, and **key words**.

Animated videos make static images come alive.

Resource icons on each page help readers to further **explore key concepts**.

Published by AV2
350 5th Avenue, 59th Floor
New York, NY 10118
Website: www.av2books.com

Library of Congress Control Number: 2019955111

ISBN 978-1-7911-2123-5 (hardcover)
ISBN 978-1-7911-2124-2 (softcover)
ISBN 978-1-7911-2125-9 (multi-user eBook)
ISBN 978-1-7911-2126-6 (single-user eBook)

Printed in Guangzhou, China
1 2 3 4 5 6 7 8 9 0 24 23 22 21 20

022020
101119

Project Coordinator: John Willis
Designer: Terry Paulhus

Every reasonable effort has been made to trace ownership and to obtain permission to reprint copyright material. The publishers would be pleased to have any errors or omissions brought to their attention so that they may be corrected in subsequent printings.

AV2 acknowledges Alamy, Getty Images, Minden Pictures, and Shutterstock as its primary image suppliers for this title.